THE VAMPIRE'S MUSE

Laura Shenton

THE VAMPIRE'S MUSE

Laura Shenton

Iridescent Toad Publishing

Iridescent Toad Publishing.

First edition. ISBN: 978-1-913779-85-6

Chapter One

The sun was low in the sky, casting a soft orange glow across the terrace where Erica sat with her mother. The sweet scent of lavender wafted through the air from the nearby garden, and a gentle breeze rustled the leaves on the trees. In this moment of tranquillity, it was difficult for Erica to imagine that anything could disrupt their idyllic life in Normandy.

"Darling," her mother said softly, interrupting the silence as she nursed her cup of tea. "There's something I need to tell you."

Erica raised an eyebrow, studying her mother's face. It had been a long time since she had seen such seriousness etched in her features.

Her mother took a deep breath as she set her teacup down with a clink. The tension in the air was palpable.

"What is it, Mother?"

"I'm getting married," she announced, unable to conceal her excitement.

"Married?!" Erica repeated, her eyes widening in shock.

Erica could hardly believe her ears. Her mother hadn't even mentioned dating anyone, let alone getting married.

"Yes," her mother replied, a faint smile playing on her lips. "His name is Derek, and he's a wonderful man. We're leaving for Rome in a few days, for a six-month honeymoon."

"Rome?"

Erica's voice caught in her throat, as if a cold hand had suddenly squeezed it.

"Yes," her mother replied. "Of course, I don't wish to pay rent on this place here while I'm away, and Derek is saving up for us to get a place together when we come back from our honeymoon. Perhaps somewhere in the States would be nice, but admittedly, we haven't decided yet."

The words struck Erica like a thunderbolt, leaving her reeling in their wake. A thousand questions swirled through her mind, each more intrusive than the last. How could this be happening? Why hadn't her mother confided in her sooner?

"But what about me?"

"Erica, my love," her mother said, reaching out to take her hand. "I wish you could come with us, but this trip, it's for Derek and me to start our lives together."

"I don't understand, Mother. What am I supposed to do while you traipse off into the sunset with this stranger?"

"Erica," her mother said firmly, her voice carrying a note of finality. "You will be going to live with your Aunt Petra and Uncle Frank in Scotland. They have a lovely estate in Burclyde, and they are eager to welcome you into their home."

"Scotland?!" Erica exclaimed, her heart sinking as she pictured the gloomy moors and endless rain, so far removed from the sun-drenched shores of Normandy. "I don't even know them!

You're sending me away to live with strangers?!"

"Darling, they are family," her mother insisted, her tone gentle yet unyielding. "You can board with them while I'm away on honeymoon. When I come back, we'll take things from there."

"Please, Mother," Erica implored, her voice cracking with emotion. "Let me go to Rome with you. I can find a job and get an apartment. I can make my own way there."

"Darling," her mother replied frankly. "Everything has been arranged. Besides, you don't speak the language. And anyway, you'd be on your own there; Derek and I are looking forward to taking lots of day trips together. It's not the right moment for you to be with us. I do hope you can see what I mean."

Erica saw only too well. Time and time again, she had been put at the whim of her mother's love life. Ever since her father had left when she was six, Erica had lived with two different stepfathers in her twenty years. Her mother's serial monogamy had always been a source of anxiety and upheaval.

Perhaps it was foolish of me to think that we would remain settled here in Normandy, Erica thought, scolding herself for having been so naive.

"Please, Mother, I'm begging you. Let me come with you."

"Erica," her mother said, her voice steady but cold. "You are a bright young woman, but you are still too immature for what Derek and I have planned. You must understand that this is an important time for us, and we cannot be saddled with a child."

The word stung as it passed through Erica's ears, igniting a fire in her chest.

"Child?!" she said indignantly. "I'm twenty years old! I'm not a child anymore!"

"Darling, you may be grown in age, but you still have so much to learn."

Her mother's gaze softened for a moment, betraying a fleeting glimpse of regret in her eyes before it vanished behind a veil of resolve.

"Scotland is so far away," Erica protested.

"Scotland is a beautiful place, my love," her mother said, attempting to quell Erica's fears. "Petra is my sister. They have plenty of room for you at their estate. It will be a wonderful opportunity for you to experience a different way of life."

Erica's mind raced, searching for any argument that might sway her mother. Deep down though, she knew it was futile.

"Can't we find a different solution? Can't I stay here on my own?"

"Erica, your Aunt Petra and Uncle Frank are more than capable of hosting you. You need to trust that I am making the best decision for all of us. Besides, it's only for six months. Time will fly by, and before you know it, you'll be complaining that you don't want to leave Scotland."

Erica doubted that very much, but her mother's tone made it clear that there was no room for debate. With the finality of her mother's decision weighing heavily upon her, Erica could only nod in agreement, her thoughts already drifting towards the unknown future that awaited her in the wilds of Scotland.

Chapter Two

The days that followed were a whirlwind of activity. Seamstresses and florists swarmed the house, their laughter mingling with the scent of fresh-cut roses and the hum of sewing machines. Erica found herself perched on a stool as her gown was adjusted, the delicate fabric like a shimmering waterfall cascading down from her shoulders. Her mother's wedding dress was a vision in ivory, its intricate pattern of pearls and lace embodying elegance and timelessness.

"Your mother will look absolutely radiant," the head seamstress declared as she stepped back to admire her handiwork. "And you, Erica, will be the belle of the ball."

"Thank you," Erica replied, her voice soft and distant.

Despite the beauty surrounding her, Erica couldn't help but feel like an unwelcome stranger in her own life.

"Are you alright, dear?" her mother asked, noticing Erica's quiet demeanour. "You seem... troubled."

"Everything is just happening so quickly," Erica confessed, her eyes welling up with unshed tears. "I'm happy for you, Mother, truly I am. It's just that everything is going to be so different for me."

The wedding passed by in a blur for Erica, and soon, the day of her mother's departure arrived. Low in the sky, the sun cast long golden shadows across the manicured lawn as the newlyweds prepared to embark on their journey. Erica watched as her mother and Derek packed the last of their luggage into the taxi, their faces aglow with happiness and anticipation.

"You'll be fine, my dear," her mother said as she brashly pulled Erica into a final embrace before quickly pulling away to climb into the waiting car.

After slamming the door shut behind her, Erica's

mother happily waggled her fingers at her daughter through the window. She then leaned in towards her new husband to plant a kiss on his cheek.

It was all too upfront for Erica. Time seemed to slow down as she stared at the gleaming black car that would whisk them away on their honeymoon.

"Goodbye, Mother," she called out, her voice barely audible above the rumble of the engine as the vehicle chugged noisily away.

And then they were gone – vanished around the bend like a dream, leaving Erica alone with her thoughts and the sinking feeling that her world had just irrevocably shifted beneath her feet.

She had no choice but to turn her attention to her own departure. She glanced around the courtyard, taking in the white stone walls and kaleidoscopic patterns of the many flowers in full bloom. How strange it felt to be leaving this place – her home for the past several years – only to be whisked away to an unfamiliar land and the hospitality of strangers.

"Miss Carmichael?"

A soft voice interrupted Erica's thoughts. She turned around to see Mrs Duval, the housekeeper, standing behind her.

"I've arranged for a car to take you to the airport. It should be here any moment."

"Thank you," Erica replied.

She attempted a smile, but her heart felt heavy, like a stone dropped into the depths of the ocean.

"Is there anything else I can do for you, dear?" Mrs Duval asked kindly, her eyes full of concern.

"No, I think I have everything," Erica said, adjusting her grip on the handle of her suitcase. "But thank you."

"Very well, then."

The housekeeper hesitated for a moment, but then reached out to give Erica a gentle pat on the arm.

"You'll be just fine, Miss Carmichael. You're stronger than you know."

"Thank you," Erica whispered, feeling the sting of tears in her eyes. "I hope so."

Just then, a sleek silver car pulled up, and the driver stepped out to greet them.

"Miss Carmichael?" he enquired, tipping his hat respectfully.

"Y-Yes, that's me."

"Allow me to take your luggage," he offered, extending his hand for her suitcase.

"Thank you," Erica replied.

She reluctantly relinquished her grip on the worn leather handle. As she watched the driver place the suitcase in the trunk of the car, she couldn't help but wonder if this was a mistake – if there was still time to change her mind or to find another solution.

"Are you ready, Miss Carmichael?" the driver asked, holding the door open for her.

No, she wanted to scream. *No, I'm not ready. I don't want to leave my home and go to live with strangers in a strange place.* But instead, she swallowed her fear and gave a small nod.

"Yes, I'm ready. Thank you."

"Very well," said the driver.

He helped her into the car and shut the door behind her. As the vehicle pulled away from the house, Erica gazed sadly out of the window, watching as the familiar landscape receded into the distance.

Chapter Three

Erica settled into the uncomfortable aeroplane seat, her gaze fixed on the shrinking Normandy landscape outside the window. Her stomach churned with a mixture of anxiety and regret as the plane gained altitude, leaving behind everything familiar to her.

"Would you like some water?" the flight attendant asked, offering a small plastic cup.

"Thank you," Erica murmured, accepting the water and taking a sip.

The cold refreshment did little to quell her growing concern. As she stared at her faint reflection in the window, Erica's thoughts swirled with uncertainty. If only she had found a job and secured an apartment in Normandy when she'd had the chance. It was infuriating that she had allowed herself to be so easily dismissed by her mother. She was twenty years old, for heaven's sake, not a child!

"Are you ok?" asked the man sitting next to her, sensing her distress.

"Fine, just... nervous," Erica replied as she forced a smile, unwilling to divulge her inner turmoil to a stranger.

"First time flying?" he enquired kindly.

"No, it's not that. I'm moving to live with relatives I've never met before," she confessed.

"Ah, I see. Well, change can be daunting, but sometimes it leads to wonderful discoveries," the man reassured her, the lines around his eyes crinkling as he smiled warmly.

"Perhaps," Erica replied, unconvinced.

She wished she could share the man's optimism, but worry clawed at her mind, leaving her feeling vulnerable and exposed.

The remainder of the flight passed in silence, save for the occasional offer of snacks and drinks from the flight attendants. As the plane began its descent, Erica glanced out the window once more in anticipation. The sprawling Scottish countryside greeted her, a patchwork quilt of green and brown, dotted with clusters of stone buildings.

"Welcome to Scotland, ladies and gentlemen," the pilot announced as the plane touched down. "We hope you enjoy your stay."

Erica gathered her belongings, her hands trembling slightly as she clutched her purse. As she disembarked from the plane and entered the bustling airport terminal, she felt a strange mixture of dread and excitement. This was it: the beginning of her new life in a foreign land.

Through the throngs of travellers, she scanned the arrivals hall for any sign of her mysterious relatives. The smell of coffee and worn leather filled the air, and the steady hum of chatter intermingled with announcements echoing throughout the terminal. Her pulse quickened, her eyes darting from face to face, searching for any flicker of recognition.

"Excuse me," she murmured to a passing airport worker. "I'm looking for someone holding up a sign, perhaps? My aunt and uncle, they should be here to meet me."

"Ah, right. Sometimes people wait over by that wall," the worker replied, pointing to a corner near the entrance. "You might have better luck if you go there."

"Thank you," Erica said, giving him a grateful smile before making her way towards the indicated area.

As she navigated through the bustling crowd, she couldn't help but feel a pang of envy at the joyful reunions taking place around her. Hugs, laughter, and excited chatter filled the space, while she remained adrift in uncertainty.

"Please be here," she whispered under her breath, hoping that her hosts would magically appear before her.

As she approached the small group of people waiting with signs, a wave of disappointment washed over her. None of the signs bore her name. She stood there for a moment, willing for just one person to materialise, yet the sea of faces remained stubbornly unfamiliar.

Her mind raced with possibilities. Had they forgotten her arrival? Had there been a miscommunication, or worse, a deliberate decision to leave her stranded? She shook her head, trying to push away the dark thoughts that threatened to swallow her whole.

Get a grip, Erica, she thought. *They'll be here. They have to be.*

With a deep breath, she resolved to wait just a little longer, hoping against hope that someone would appear and put an end to her mounting anxiety. But as the minutes ticked by and the crowd around her thinned, the disheartening truth became harder to ignore: she was alone in a strange new place, with no one waiting to welcome her home.

"Could they have left a message?" she wondered aloud.

She nervously approached the airport information desk.

"Excuse me," she stammered, catching the attention of the uniformed attendant. "I'm looking for my aunt and uncle, Petra and Frank Laramie. They were supposed to meet me here.

Is there any chance they left a message for me?"

"I'll just check for you," the attendant replied with a polite smile.

The woman deftly shuffled through a pile of neatly-arranged papers, her manicured nails occasionally reflecting the artificial lighting all around. Erica held her breath, her fingers toying nervously with the strap of her handbag.

"I'm afraid there are no messages for you," the attendant informed her apologetically. "I'm sorry."

"Thank you," Erica mumbled, her shoulders slumping in defeat.

"Is everything alright, dear?" an elderly gentleman asked as he walked up beside her, his bushy eyebrows furrowed in concern.

"I... I don't know," Erica admitted, tears prickling at the corners of her eyes. "I'm supposed to be meeting my aunt and uncle, but they're not here, and I don't know what to do."

"Perhaps they're just running late," the man suggested gently. "Why don't you have a seat and give them a few more minutes? I'm sure they'll turn up."

"Maybe," Erica agreed, forcing a weak smile.

She couldn't shake the feeling that something was amiss, but all she could do was take a seat on the cold metal bench as her thoughts whirled. Acutely aware of her vulnerability in this strange new environment, Erica clutched her small suitcase tightly, as if it were an anchor against the tide of confusion that threatened to sweep her away.

Perhaps I should call them, she decided, her gaze catching sight of a row of payphones across the terminal.

With purposeful strides, she navigated through the throngs of travellers who had just arrived from another flight.

As she approached the phones, however, she was met with disappointment. One of them hung limply off the hook, its casing cracked and broken. The other appeared to be functional, but when she opened her purse to retrieve some change, she realised she didn't have the right currency.

"Of course," she muttered, frustration evident in her tone. "Just my luck."

She scanned the area, hoping to find someone who could help her, but the faces that met her gaze were either too busy or too disinterested to notice her plight.

Despite her apprehension, Erica steeled herself and approached a middle-aged woman with a friendly face.

"Excuse me," she said, her voice quivering slightly. "I'm sorry to bother you, but do you happen to have any change for the phone?"

"Sorry, dear," the woman replied sincerely. "I've just used the last of my coins."

"Thank you anyway," Erica said, crestfallen, but not wishing to appear rude.

She turned her attention to a group of young men in business suits, hoping their professional attire indicated an inclination to help.

"Hi, could one of you spare some change for the phone?"

"Sure, no problem," one of the men replied.

He rummaged through his pockets, and then handed her the coins. Erica felt a surge of gratitude.

"Thank you so much," she said, clutching the coins tightly in her hand.

"Good luck with that call," he said, nodding towards the phone.

Erica returned to the payphone, her spirits lifted by this small act of kindness. She had barely started dialling when a tall man with dark hair and brown eyes appeared beside her.

"Miss Carmichael?" he asked, his deep voice resonating with certainty.

"Y-yes?" Erica stammered, taken aback by his sudden appearance.

"Forgive my intrusion," he said, offering a slight bow. "My name is Robert Hulme. The Laramies sent me to collect you. They were unable to make it themselves due to unforeseen circumstances."

"What happened?" Erica queried, her curiosity piqued.

"I'm not sure if it's my place to say so, but it's nothing you need to worry about," he answered. "Rest assured though, I am here to ensure that you arrive safely to the Laramie estate."

As Robert's eyes met hers, Erica detected a glimmer of concern beneath his polished exterior.

"Thank you," she said, uncertainty clouding her thoughts.

She hesitated for a moment before looking around for the man who had so kindly given her change for the phone. Unable to spot him, and assuming that he must have left, she carefully put the coins in her purse.

"Please, allow me to carry your luggage," Robert offered, extending his hand. "It's only a short walk to the car, but you must be tired from your journey."

"Alright," Erica agreed as she handed him her suitcase.

She followed him out of the airport and, as they walked, she reasoned that he seemed genuine enough. Besides, with no other options available, she had no choice but to put her trust in him.

30

Chapter Four

The car, a sleek black vehicle of indeterminate make, hummed smoothly as it made its way along the winding roads of rural Scotland. Rain danced upon the windows, blurring the landscape beyond into a hazy mirage. Erica sank into the plush leather seat, her eyes darting between the passing countryside and the man who had come to collect her.

"Forgive me for prying, but what brings you to Scotland," Robert enquired, casting a sidelong glance at Erica.

"Truthfully, I didn't have much choice," she confessed, her gaze falling to her lap. "My mother is... well, she's rather self-centred and aloof. She's on her honeymoon with her third husband, and I suppose I was just... in the way."

Erica knew her words were laced with bitterness, and so she quickly tried to mask her feelings with a shrug.

"I see," Robert murmured, his expression thoughtful. "Family matters can be... complicated."

Intrigued but not wishing to pry, Erica nodded and turned her attention to the rolling hills outside the window. The rain intensified, drumming an erratic rhythm against the car's roof.

"How do you know the Laramies?" she asked, attempting to lighten the mood.

"Ah, well," Robert replied, shifting gears and casting her a quick glance filled with a hint of amusement. "I'm an accountant by trade. I manage their finances and help run the household."

"An accountant?" Erica asked, arching an eyebrow.

"Yeah," he said, his eyes focused on the slick road ahead. "I've been with the Laramies for a few years now, and I spend quite a bit of time at the estate. You see, I'm involved with Constance – Petra and Frank's daughter."

"Constance," Erica repeated the name, filing it away in her memory.

"Yes," Robert confirmed. "The family have more rooms than occupants. There's just Frank, Petra, Constance and Jack who live there. There's plenty of room for you at the house. Oh, and the housekeeper, Mrs McGinnon – she's pleasant enough. I must say though, be careful of the company you choose to keep."

He offered no further elaboration, which only served to heighten Erica's anxiety.

"What do you mean?" she asked, annoyed that Robert was being so cryptic.

He frowned, a troubled expression flitting across his face.

"I wish I could provide you with concrete answers, Erica, really I do. But some things are better left unsaid. Trust your instincts and tread carefully."

Erica's curiosity was piqued despite the

churning unease in her gut. It was as if the very air around them had grown heavy with unspoken words.

"Come on," Robert said, releasing a frustrated sigh, as though he had been forbidden to elaborate. "I don't mean to alarm you, but I would be remiss if I didn't express my concern for your wellbeing. Just keep your wits about you, and if you ever need assistance, do not hesitate to call on me."

"Thank you," Erica conceded, touched by his earnestness, but still concerned.

The storm raged around them, casting shadows across the landscape. As they neared their destination, the rain fell heavier, the drumming against the car roof drowning out all other sounds.

"There's a shortcut to the Laramie estate that not many people know about," Robert said, his voice steady and calm despite the chaos outside. "It follows a road near the cliffside and will save us some time. Would you like me to take it?"

"Sure," Erica replied, her voice wavering slightly as she imagined the perilous route. "As long as it's safe."

"Of course," Robert assured her, his tone confident.

As they turned onto the narrow road, Erica wasn't sure what to think. The wind howled around them, and the cliffs seemed to loom menacingly before the charcoal sky. The headlights struggled to penetrate the thick dusk that had enveloped the car as it continued along the winding road.

"We're nearly there now," Robert announced, his voice a reassuring baritone. "The Laramie estate is just ahead."

As they rounded a final bend, Erica caught sight of the imposing estate through the rain-streaked window. Her eyes widened in awe at the grandeur of the ancient manor house. It was partially obscured by fog, but she could make out an ornate iron gate and the stone walls surrounding the property. She thought she could see the faint outlines of statues dotting the lawn leading up to the entrance – like sentinels guarding a long-held secret.

"Those statues," she said, unable to suppress her

admiration. "They're impressive."

"Indeed," Robert replied, casting a sidelong glance at her. "Jack has a particular talent for capturing the essence of his subjects in stone."

"That's amazing."

With a soft rumble, the car rolled to a stop within the estate grounds, the headlights illuminating the family waiting for them outside: two men and two women, their faces difficult to read. Erica's breath hitched in her throat – she had a feeling that her life was about to change forever.

"The Laramies," Robert confirmed, noticing her questioning gaze. "Petra and Frank – your aunt and uncle – and Constance and Jack."

"Thank you, Robert," she said, her heart pounding in anticipation of meeting her enigmatic relatives.

"Please remember what I said earlier about being cautious," Robert said, his voice deep with concern. "You never know where danger might lie."

"Of course," Erica replied, trying to sound confident despite the knot in her stomach.

She took a deep breath, steeling herself for the encounter ahead. As she reached for the car door handle, she hoped that her curiosity and intelligence would be enough to help her navigate her stay at the Laramie estate. With one final glance at Robert, she opened the door and stepped out into the rain to greet her hosts.

Chapter Five

The first thing that struck Erica as she stepped out of the car was the sombre atmosphere that hung in the air like a thick fog. She gazed upon her Aunt Petra, Uncle Frank, and their two adult children. They were all dressed in mourning attire, their faces etched with grief. Erica's heart sank at the realisation that there must have been a death.

"Erica, dear," Aunt Petra said, her voice strained but steady. "I'm afraid we've just returned from a funeral. Someone from the nearby village passed away quite suddenly."

"Oh," Erica uttered. "I'm sorry to hear that."

"As am I," Aunt Petra replied evasively, her piercing gaze conveying a silent plea for Erica not to press further.

Sensing her aunt's unwillingness to elaborate, Erica nodded in understanding, though her curiosity remained piqued, gnawing at the edges of her consciousness.

Constance then stepped forwards, her red hair cascading down her shoulders like a fiery waterfall – it framed her delicate face, adorned with freckles. The young woman's eyes were rimmed with red, evidence of her recent tears, but she managed a small welcoming smile as she approached Erica.

"Hello Erica," she said, her voice giving away the slight apprehension in her demeanour. "It's nice to meet you."

"Nice to meet you too, Constance," Erica replied.

Commanding the space, Jack stepped forward, his dark hair slicked back and his intense gaze seeming to bore into Erica's soul. There was an air of mystery about him. His handsome features and strong jawline only served to add to the enigma.

"Erica," he said, his voice deep and resonant. "I'm Jack. It's a pleasure to meet you."

"Likewise," Erica replied cautiously, sensing there was something about him that she just couldn't put her finger on.

Uncle Frank then reached out to shake her hand, his tall frame stooping slightly. His grip was warm but distant, and she noticed the subtle trembling of his fingers as they brushed against her palm. The faint scent of cigar smoke clung to his well-tailored suit, and beneath the surface of his friendly smile, she could sense an underlying sadness that seemed to weigh heavily upon him.

"Welcome, Erica," he said, attempting a reassuring tone. "I'm glad you finally made it here."

"Thank you, Uncle Frank," she replied, trying not to let the uncertainty show on her face. "I'm sorry for your loss."

"Ah, yes," he said with a sigh, looking away for a moment before continuing. "It's been a trying time for us all."

"Come along now," Aunt Petra said, swiftly changing the subject and gesturing for Erica to follow her.

From the outside, the imposing mansion was more daunting than Erica could have imagined, its towering spires reaching towards the darkening sky. She felt a shiver run down her spine, but she pushed her reservations aside as she began to follow her aunt and uncle, with Constance and Jack following along behind her.

The creaking of the massive oak doors echoed ominously through the cavernous space, their shadows casting shapes on the aged marble floor. Having parked the car, Robert closed the heavy doors behind him and proceeded to follow along behind everyone else.

Erica's footsteps seemed to reverberate as she stepped forwards, her eyes darting around to take in the opulent surroundings. As they walked through the dimly lit halls, she couldn't help but notice the tension that clung to the family like a second skin. It was an almost palpable force, filling the air with a sense of foreboding.

"Thank you for taking me in," she told her aunt, attempting to establish a rapport.

"It's ok, Erica," Aunt Petra replied, her voice strained with the effort of maintaining composure. "It's just been a difficult day for us all."

"Is there anything I can do?" Erica offered.

"Thank you, dear," Aunt Petra said, her eyes softening ever so slightly. "But there's nothing anyone can do now. We must simply carry on."

As they stepped into the drawing room, a curious sight caught Erica's attention. A white highland terrier lay on a lush velvet chaise, his small frame swaddled in an embroidered shawl. His breathing was laboured, each exhale accompanied by a pitiful wheeze.

"Is he alright?" Erica asked, her brow furrowing with concern as she approached the ailing pup.

"I'm afraid not, dear," Aunt Petra replied, woefully shaking her head. "He's been like this for days, and we're at a loss for what to do."

"Have you taken him to the vet?" Robert interjected, his gaze shifting from the dog to Aunt Petra.

"Of course I have," Jack snapped, shoving his way forward to be closer to the dog. "They couldn't find anything wrong with Tiny."

He stroked Tiny's scruffy head, and the dog

leaned into his touch, seeking comfort.

"Maybe a second opinion would be helpful," Robert suggested, trying to hide the unease that crept into his voice.

"Perhaps you're right, Robert," Aunt Petra conceded, her eyes narrowing as she considered his words. "We can't just stand by and do nothing while our dear Tiny suffers."

"Allow me to take care of it," Jack insisted, his voice smooth and persuasive. "I'll make arrangements for another veterinarian tomorrow. I won't rest until Tiny is well again."

"Thank you, Jack," Aunt Petra said gratefully, relief flickering across her face. "You know how much Tiny means to us all."

From observing the exchange, Erica was unable to shake the feeling that there was more to Jack than met the eye.

"Erica, why don't you let Constance show you around?" Aunt Petra proposed. "It'll help clear your head after such an exhausting journey."

"Of course," Erica replied. "Thank you, Aunt

Petra."

Eager for a reprieve from the mounting tension, Erica followed Constance out of the drawing room, but she couldn't help but glance back at Tiny once more.

The two young women wandered off together, their footsteps echoing against the marble flooring within the spacious hallways. Erica couldn't help but notice the strain that seemed to follow them like a shadow. As they made their way through the labyrinthine corridors, her curiosity began to get the better of her. There was something about the Laramie family that tugged at her, a sense of disarray that she couldn't ignore.

"Constance," she whispered cautiously. "I can't help but notice the tension between everyone."

"Erica, I..." Constance hesitated, her gaze shifting away from Erica's probing stare. "It's... it's just been a difficult day, that's all."

Erica scolded herself for having been so nosy. Not only was their beloved dog poorly, but the family had just been to a funeral and were still in their mourning clothes.

"I'm sorry," she said. "I didn't mean to pry."

"It's ok," said Constance. "Everything here is new to you. I understand that you must feel nervous."

"You're right," said Erica. "It was such a shock when Mother announced that I would be staying here with you in Scotland."

"I know it's probably a lot to take in at first," Constance offered, her voice soft and gentle. "Don't worry though, Erica. You can tell me anything; I'll do everything I can to make sure you're ok here. There's no need to be afraid."

"I'm not afraid, I just..."

Erica allowed her voice to trail off. She hadn't mentioned anything about being afraid. It felt odd to her that Constance had assumed as much.

Chapter Six

"Shall we head upstairs?" Constance asked, her voice soft and welcoming. "I could show you to your room, if you like?"

"Of course," Erica replied.

She glanced over to the opulent staircase that led to the upper floors of the large house, and couldn't help but feel a sense of awe at the grandeur surrounding her.

As they walked up the stairs, the light from the late afternoon sun filtered in through the stained glass windows, casting an array of colours onto the walls. Erica tried to take in every detail, from the elaborate tapestries depicting scenes of countryside hunting history, to the ornate chandeliers that hung above them.

"Your room is on the third floor," Constance

explained as they continued upwards. "The house is rather large, so I'm afraid I won't be able to give you a full tour today. But please, make yourself comfortable, and don't hesitate to explore on your own."

"Thank you," Erica said.

The number of doors lining the hallways seemed to be endless. Erica wondered what lay behind them all, and how many of the rooms had been left undisturbed for years, perhaps even decades.

The pair stopped before an intricately-carved door adorned with brass fittings.

"Here we are," Constance announced as she turned the key.

As soon as Constance pushed the door open, Erica was met with a sight that took her breath away. The room was beautiful – a perfect blend of aged elegance and modern comfort. Heavy velvet drapes framed the tall windows, offering a view of the sprawling estate below, whilst a magnificent canopy bed stood as the centrepiece of the space, draped in rich silks and embroidered linens. Faded wallpaper clung to the walls, its pattern reminiscent of blooming roses, and a grand fireplace lay dormant, its mantel adorned with antique trinkets and photographs.

An abundance of old-but-sturdy furniture filled the space – a towering mahogany wardrobe, a writing desk with a delicate silver inkwell, and an ornate vanity table laden with jewel-encrusted brushes and mirrors. The air was heavy with the scent of lavender and beeswax, mingling with the musty trace of age-old secrets.

"Wow," Erica murmured, her eyes darting around the room in wonder. "This is incredible."

"I'm glad you like it," Constance said with a smile, clearly pleased with Erica's reaction. "I hope you'll feel at home here."

"Thank you," Erica replied sincerely.

Despite the unsettling undercurrents she had sensed within the Laramie family, her cousin's warmth and kindness shone through.

"Would you like me to help you unpack?" Constance offered, gesturing towards the suitcase that had been brought up earlier.

"That's kind of you," Erica said gratefully. "Yes please."

As the two women placed Erica's clothes in a nearby drawer, even amongst their cheerful small talk, a sense of disquiet settled over Erica. The room was undeniably beautiful, but she couldn't dismiss the feeling that there were memories clinging to every surface like dust. She shivered, trying to dispel the sense of trepidation that prickled her skin.

"We should probably head down for dinner," said Constance as she closed Erica's emptied suitcase. "I bet you're hungry."

Not wishing to draw attention to the fact that nobody had offered her so much as a biscuit or a cup of tea since her arrival, Erica smiled and nodded with enthusiasm.

The dining room was no less impressive than the rest of the house. It had a long mahogany table polished to a high shine, which was surrounded by high-backed chairs upholstered in emerald-green velvet. The rest of the Laramie family had already taken their seats, and each member wore their own particular expression: Aunt Petra's eyes sparkled with authority, Uncle Frank looked lost in his own thoughts, and Jack's gaze seemed cold and challenging.

"Ah, there you are, dear," Aunt Petra said to Erica, gesturing for her to take a seat next to Constance, who happily sat down next to Robert.

The dinner progressed with an air of tense politeness. Conversation was stilted and forced, punctuated by moments of awkward silence. Erica quickly noticed that the only interaction that seemed natural and comfortable was when Constance's attention drifted towards Robert – her admiring eyes lingering on him, her lips curving into a soft, wistful smile, her fingers fiddling nervously with the stem of her wine glass.

"This room is beautiful, Aunt Petra," Erica said, trying to break the uncomfortable silence.

"Thank you, dear," Aunt Petra responded, her tone firm, yet proud.

Uncle Frank mumbled something to himself as he stared down at his plate. The weight of his passivity left Erica feeling oddly saddened.

"Jack, don't forget about Tiny's appointment tomorrow," Aunt Petra reminded, her tone sharp enough to cut glass.

Jack merely nodded, his gaze never straying far from Erica.

As dinner continued, the family dynamics seemed to unravel before Erica's eyes. No conversation flowed naturally, each word carefully chosen, as though they all walked on eggshells. Erica watched the family's interactions, and couldn't help but feel like an intruder in their world.

"Would anyone care for dessert?" a rotund woman announced, presenting a silver tray laden with delicate cakes and pastries.

Taking her cue from everyone else at the table, Erica accepted a slice of cake that looked almost too beautiful to eat. With each bite, she hoped to find some sweetness to counteract the bitter atmosphere.

As she speared the final morsel of cake with her fork, she couldn't get past the unsettling feeling that she was being watched. The rich flavours of the dessert had momentarily distracted her from the awkward ambience, but now that her plate lay empty, she couldn't ignore it any longer.

Her eyes scanned the room for the source of her discomfort, her focus darting between the family members seated around the table – Uncle Frank staring blankly at his untouched dessert, Constance still stealing glances at Robert, and Aunt Petra's hardened expression.

It wasn't until her gaze fell upon Jack that she discovered the reason for her unease. He sat across the table, his dark eyes locked onto her with an intensity that caused her to shudder. There was something about him that seemed both alluring and dangerous, like a hidden trap waiting to ensnare its prey.

"Jack," Aunt Petra said, turning her attention to him with an air of annoyance in her tone. "Would you be so good as to go and check on Tiny for us, please?"

"Of course," Jack acquiesced, his voice smooth and charming despite the intensity in his expression.

He rose from his seat, sparing one last lingering

look at Erica before he left the room.

"Now then," Aunt Petra announced, rising almost ceremonially from her seat. "Would you like me to show you more of the house, Erica?"

"Yes, please," Erica replied, certain that she had little choice in the matter.

"Very well," Aunt Petra confirmed. "Follow me."

The older woman's heels clicked sharply against the polished marble floor as they made their way through the vast corridors. The walls were adorned with oil paintings that seemed to watch their every move, their subjects eternally trapped within the confines of their gilded frames.

"Here is our library," Aunt Petra proudly declared.

She pushed open the heavy oak doors to reveal a cavernous room filled with floor-to-ceiling bookshelves lining every wall. Their contents ranged from ancient tomes bound in cracked leather, to modern paperbacks. The air was heavy with the scent of old paper and ink, mingling with a hint of mildew.

"Wow, it's incredible," said Erica, trying to take in each detail.

She imagined herself lost in the pages of a good book. She had always enjoyed reading back in Normandy, especially out on the terrace on a gentle summer's day.

"I'm sure it will take a while for you to find your way around the estate," Aunt Petra explained. "But of course, you're always welcome to visit the library any time you like."

"Thank you," said Erica, feeling inspired.

"Well," said Aunt Petra. "Let's head back to the dining room. I would like to speak to Robert before everyone turns in for the night."

Back in the dining room, Uncle Frank was nursing a drink, whilst Constance and Robert talked amongst themselves.

"Robert," Aunt Petra announced. "Let's talk about those figures we were discussing earlier, shall we?"

Politely excusing himself from Constance, Robert graciously followed along after Aunt Petra. Erica then sat next to Constance to keep her company.

"Did Mother tell you about Jack's studio at the end of the garden?" Constance asked suddenly, her voice hushed as if sharing a secret. "He spends most of his time out there, working on his sculptures."

"She didn't mention it," Erica answered.

Her curiosity was piqued – both by the mention of Jack's studio, and the subtle note of apprehension in Constance's voice.

"Jack is... talented," Constance admitted, biting her lip. "But there's something about his work that makes people uncomfortable. The family tends to avoid his studio."

"Uncomfortable how?" Erica pressed, sensing that there was more to the story than Constance was letting on.

"His sculptures are... intense," Constance hesitated, as if searching for the right words. "They seem to capture something deep within the soul – something dark and primal. It's hard to describe, but once you've seen them, it's difficult to shake off the feeling they evoke."

"I noticed the sculptures outside. They caught my eye straight away when I first arrived."

"What did you think of them?" Constance asked, a hint of urgency in her voice.

"They were ok," Erica replied, not quite sure of what Constance wanted her to say.

As Erica's mind wandered to thoughts of what could be so awful about Jack's studio, a sudden rustle behind her made her jump. Turning around, she found Jack standing there, cradling Tiny in his arms as if he had materialised out of thin air. His intense stare bored into her, and she couldn't help but shudder.

"Ah, so you've heard about my studio," he said, his voice smooth and low. "You're welcome to visit anytime, Erica."

"Thank you," she replied warily.

Constance's words still echoed in her mind, making her feel both curious and apprehensive.

"Jack is an incredibly talented sculptor," Constance added, her tone shifting from nervousness to admiration. "His work is truly one-of-a-kind."

"Indeed," Jack agreed, a hint of pride creeping into his voice. "I find inspiration in the darkest corners of life, channelling it into my art."

"Dark corners?" Erica queried, her eyes narrowing with suspicion.

She couldn't help but wonder what secrets Jack was hiding behind his enigmatic façade.

"Ah, yes," he responded, a sly smile curling the corners of his lips. "I won't spoil the surprise for you. You'll have to see for yourself."

Erica couldn't overcome the feeling that Jack's interest in her went beyond mere curiosity. It felt like he was probing her, trying to gauge her reactions. What did he want from her? And why was something as innocuous as a sculpting studio shrouded in so much mystery?

"Jack, perhaps we should leave Erica to get settled for the night," Constance suggested, sensing Erica's discomfort.

"Of course," Jack conceded.

His gaze lingered on Erica for a moment longer before he turned away. As he walked towards the door with Tiny nestled in his arms, there was something in his demeanour that unsettled Erica deeply.

"Goodnight, Erica," he called over his shoulder, disappearing into the shadows of the hallway.

As the evening drew to an end, Erica's thoughts swirled with unanswered questions and veiled warnings. The Laramie family's strange nature was beginning to weigh on her, leaving her more uncertain than ever.

60

Chapter Seven

The moonlight streamed in through the narrow slit between the velvet curtains, casting a silver glow upon the antique four-poster bed. Erica lay in its embrace, her chestnut hair splayed out across the pillow like a silken fan. Her breaths came slow and steady as she drifted on the edge of sleep, but an uneasy feeling gnawed at her subconscious, tethering her to wakefulness.

"Erica," whispered a baritone voice that seemed to emanate from the shadows themselves.

Her eyes snapped open. Her heart raced like a wild stallion, pounding against the cage of her ribs. As she listened intensively for any sound beyond the whisper of wind outside, the room remained unnaturally still.

"Erica…" the voice called again, more insistent

this time, sending tendrils of icy dread down her spine.

She gripped the sheets tightly, her knuckles white with the effort. Was it her imagination playing tricks on her?

"Who's there?" she demanded boldly, her voice quivering slightly despite her best efforts.

Silence answered her challenge, mocking her with its emptiness. She took several deep steadying breaths, trying to convince herself that the male voice was just a figment of her overactive imagination. However, the lingering dread refused to be banished so easily.

As she strained to see any hint of movement amongst the gloom, the breath of another seemed to emanate from every direction, an omnipresent threat lurking just out of sight.

"Erica..." the voice whispered again, its tone insidious and chilling.

Gathering her wits, Erica forced herself to sit up, her eyes scanning the room in search of the elusive source of the voice. Nothing stirred; the only sound was the distant howling of the wind outside, a mournful accompaniment to her mounting dread.

"Show yourself!" she demanded, desperate for some semblance of control over the situation.

Her eyes darted from corner to corner, searching for any sign of life amidst the oppressive shadows, but the room remained obstinately empty, mocking her with its silence.

"Erica..." the voice persisted, taunting her with its proximity, yet remaining maddeningly elusive.

It was as though it was right beside her, breathing heavily into her ear, tickling her soft skin with its vibrato.

"Stop it!" she shouted, anger bubbling up within to combat her growing fear.

She couldn't understand why this was happening to her. What had she done to deserve such torment? The voice seemed intent on driving her mad, pushing her further and further into a pit of despair.

"Leave me alone!" she pleaded.

She buried her face in her hands. She felt utterly powerless, a helpless victim at the mercy of an unseen tormentor. The voice chuckled darkly, feeding on her anguish like a ravenous beast.

"Erica..." it whispered, its tone laced with malevolent satisfaction.

Erica's scream tore through the stillness of the night, a piercing cry that shattered the darkness. Her heart hammered as she clutched the bedsheets, her eyes wide and wild with terror.

"Erica!"

She was startled to hear the sound of a different voice – one without malice. She looked up to see Uncle Frank and Aunt Petra standing in the doorway, their faces pale and anxious. She could see the concern in Uncle Frank's eyes, but Aunt Petra's were hard and unreadable.

"Someone... someone was calling my name," Erica stammered, her voice trembling. "But there's no one here."

"Darling, you're probably just tired from your long journey," Aunt Petra said dismissively, offering a tight smile that didn't quite reach her piercing eyes. "Everything seems strange and new when you're in an unfamiliar place. You'll feel better in the morning."

"Are you sure you didn't just have a nightmare?" Uncle Frank suggested gently, his warm demeanour almost masking the sadness that seemed to cling to him like a shroud. "We all have them sometimes."

"Maybe," Erica conceded reluctantly, feeling a flush of embarrassment creep along her cheeks.

Deep down, she doubted that she'd been having a mere dream. The terror had been too real, the voice too insistent.

"Get some sleep, dear," Aunt Petra instructed, her tone making it clear that the discussion was over. "We'll see you for breakfast in the morning."

With that, she turned on her heel and swept out of the room with her husband following loyally behind.

Alone in the room once more, with her swirling thoughts and unanswered questions, Erica sank back onto the pillow, her fingers tracing the delicate embroidery of the sheets. The coldness of the room seemed to close in around her, the shadows taking on sinister shapes in the corners of her vision. She couldn't dispel the notion that something was terribly wrong, and that the voice she had heard was not only real, but wanting for something.

Presently, all she could hear was the distant sigh of the wind through the trees outside, their skeletal branches casting bleak patterns against the wallpaper where fragments of moonlight made it possible. As she lay there, her thoughts racing and her heart heavy with dread, Erica couldn't help but wonder if she would ever be able to feel at ease in her strange new home.

Chapter Eight

The first light of dawn filtered through the heavy drapes, casting a pale blue hue across Erica's bedroom. As she lay in bed, her eyes wide and alert, the memory of the chilling voice echoed in her mind. Determined to uncover the truth, she rose and dressed quickly, donning a simple cotton dress that was both modest and comfortable.

Silently, she eased open the bedroom door and stepped out into the dimly lit hallway. The house seemed different in the cold light of day. Her curiosity piqued, she ventured further, her footsteps echoing softly on the polished floor.

"You're up early, dear," a voice called out suddenly from behind her.

Erica quickly spun around to find the housekeeper standing there, her plump face soft with concern.

"I couldn't sleep," Erica said nervously, her hand resting instinctively on her chest. "I thought I'd take a look around the house."

"You'll get no judgement from me," the woman said kindly. "It's not the easiest house to get a good night's sleep in, that's for sure."

"Oh?" Erica mused, sensing that the woman knew more.

"I'm Mrs McGinnon, by the way," said the woman, her tone lighter as she held out a pudgy hand in greeting. "You need not keep any secrets from me. I've seen it all."

"What do you mean?"

"Well, you must be careful, my dear," Mrs McGinnon replied, her brow furrowing. "Strange things have been known to happen here at the Laramie estate."

"Strange things?"

Mrs McGinnon hesitated, her eyes darting to the side as if searching for the right words.

"I cannot say more. I trust you'll understand that I mustn't betray the conditions of my employment; jobs are scarce around here. But trust me when I tell you that it would be in your best interests to leave this place."

"Leave?!" Erica exclaimed, taken aback by the sudden warning. "But why? What's going on here?"

"Please, just trust me," Mrs McGinnon implored, her voice low and urgent. "You are in danger here, and I do not wish to see you come to any harm."

Erica's mind raced as she tried to reconcile the housekeeper's words with what she had experienced in the night. Could there be a connection? Or was this simply another piece in the ever-growing puzzle that seemed to surround the Laramie estate?

"Please tell me what you mean," Erica whispered, her tone laced with desperation.

"I wish I could," the housekeeper said with a sigh, her kindly features drawn with regret. "But please believe me when I say that I really can't say any more. Besides, I have my own wellbeing to consider."

Before Erica could press further, the distant ringing of a church bell echoed from afar.

"Anyway," announced Mrs McGinnon, appearing grateful for the distraction. "It'll be time for breakfast soon. Put your best face on and go downstairs to join the others."

Erica couldn't help but notice that Mrs McGinnon's attempt at a reassuring smile looked anything but effortless; behind her wise, soulful eyes was not only a sadness, but a sense of urgency that spoke volumes.

Not wishing to make demands of the woman who had shown concern for her, Erica nodded politely and then made her way downstairs, her every step heavy with the weight of unanswered questions and unspoken warnings.

Upon her entry to the dining room, she was met with an atmosphere thick with tension. The Laramie family sat around the long table, the silence between them almost overwhelming. Erica hesitated for a moment before taking her place, her eyes flickering from one solemn face to another.

"Good morning everyone," she greeted cautiously, her voice low and unsteady.

"Good morning Erica," Uncle Frank responded with forced cheerfulness, his eyes betraying a deep extent of worry.

Aunt Petra offered a tight-lipped smile, her gaze darting nervously around the room.

It was then that Jack spoke up.

"I have some unfortunate news," he said with certainty and restraint. "Tiny passed away during the night."

"He was such a dear little companion," Constance said softly, dabbing at her eyes with a lace handkerchief. "He was only six. We thought he would be with us for many years to come."

"Indeed," agreed Uncle Frank, his voice tight with barely-contained emotion. "He was a healthy, rambunctious little fellow. It's simply... incomprehensible."

As the family continued their breakfast, Erica couldn't help but feel the oppressive atmosphere bearing down upon her. She took small bites of her meal, each morsel tasting like ash in her mouth.

"I shall bury Tiny today," said Jack, his voice firm and authoritative as he addressed Constance. "I would appreciate it if you and Erica could accompany me for this."

"Robert was supposed to come by today," Constance protested, her voice hesitant and strained. "I thought I might join him in town for some shopping."

There was an almost desperate note in her tone. It couldn't be doubted that Constance was devastated by the news of Tiny's death, but still she seemed wary of participating in his burial.

"Go with Jack, Constance," Uncle Frank cut in.

He shot his daughter a knowing glance, leaving her no choice but to acquiesce. His eyes held a subtle warning, making it clear that this was not a matter for debate.

Constance conceded with a nod of her head, her shoulders slumping in defeat. She turned to Erica, her gaze pleading for understanding.

"I suppose we should go with Jack, then," she said.

As they rose from the table, Erica couldn't help but observe the power dynamics at play. Despite not being the head of the household, Jack seemed to wield a significant amount of control over the family. It was an unsettling realisation, and one that she couldn't quite understand.

74

Chapter Nine

Under the garden's leafy elms, Jack, Constance, and Erica stood in a small circle. Constance clutched a small bundle in her arms – a pristine white cloth that shrouded Tiny's fragile body. The golden sunlight filtered through the lush canopy above them, casting dappled shadows on their faces. The main mansion loomed in the distance, its grand façade now just a blurred silhouette. The air was filled with the scent of damp earth and dew-kissed grass, but there was an undercurrent of unease that prickled at Erica's senses.

"Tiny had been acting quite lethargic these past few days," Constance said, her red hair framing her freckled face as she looked down at the dog's lifeless body. "But I can't understand why he died. He was perfectly fine before."

"Death is natural," Jack replied dismissively, his

dark eyes flickering with a strange intensity. "It's part of life. We are all destined to embrace it sooner or later. It's a beautiful thing, really."

Erica shifted her weight from one foot to the other, feeling the damp grass beneath her shoes. She caught herself glancing back at the distant mansion as if seeking refuge. She couldn't help but notice how Jack seemed almost enchanted by the concept of death.

"Jack, I know you're trying to help, but it doesn't make it any easier," Constance said quietly, her voice choked with emotion. "Tiny was so full of life, and now he's just... gone."

"Of course," Jack agreed, a hint of impatience in his voice. "But dwelling on his demise won't bring him back. Everything that lives must die."

Noticing as Jack's gaze moved pointedly towards her, Erica swallowed hard as she tried to ignore the discomfort that settled over her like a thick fog. What was it about Jack that made her feel so on edge? Was it his intense stare, or his morbid fascination with death?

She deliberately turned her attention to the towering elms surrounding them. With their gnarled branches reaching out like skeletal hands, she couldn't help but think that this place would be especially haunting at night. A shiver ran down her spine, and she wrapped her arms around herself, seeking comfort in the warmth of her own embrace.

"Let's just bury Tiny and try to move on," Constance suggested with a small sniffle, wiping away the tears that threatened to spill down her cheeks.

"Very well," Jack agreed, his gaze still fixed on Erica as if trying to decipher her thoughts. "We shall lay our dear friend to rest."

Jack's hands clung to the shovel as he carved a small rectangular hole in the earth. He then dug with a confident stoicism.

"Give him to me," he told Constance, his arms outstretched.

Constance hesitated, her grip tightening around Tiny's concealed body, as though she feared letting go would sever their connection forever. It was clear that she dreaded what must come next. With no choice in the matter, she reluctantly handed over the small bundle, her fingers lingering on the cloth for a moment before releasing their hold.

As Jack lowered Tiny into the grave, Erica felt an odd sense of detachment. She had known the little terrier for such a short time, yet she couldn't deny her sadness. She found herself wondering if this was how death always felt – sudden, inexplicable, and somehow deeply personal.

"Would you like to say a few words?" Jack asked, glancing at Constance, and then at Erica.

"Goodbye Tiny," Constance whispered, struggling to maintain her composure. "You brought us so much joy. I hope you find peace."

Jack nodded solemnly, taking a handful of earth and sprinkling it over Tiny's still form. He seemed almost unfazed by the act, as though he were simply tending to one of the many plants that adorned the estate. Erica watched him, her thoughts still a whirlwind of confusion and uncertainty.

"Goodbye Tiny," she echoed, adding her own handful of earth to the grave.

She wished that she had something more profound to say, but the words eluded her. Instead, she focused on the simple act of burying the small creature, hoping that it would bring some semblance of closure to the terrible loss.

With each movement of dirt, the weight of the moment seemed to grow heavier.

Once the ground was finally level, Jack picked up a small stone figure of Tiny that he had sculpted in advance. He placed it gently at the head of the grave, a final tribute to the beloved pet.

"Since we're already out here," he said suddenly, his gaze flicking towards Erica, "why don't I show you around? This part of the estate is quite beautiful, especially at this time of day."

Constance looked surprised at the suggestion, glancing between Jack and Erica with uncertainty.

"Oh, I don't know if that's necessary, Jack," she protested weakly. "Erica only came to help us bury Tiny; she doesn't need to see everything."

"Ah, but I insist," Jack replied smoothly, the

shadows beneath the elms seeming to deepen as he spoke. "We can't have our dear guest leave without a proper tour, now can we?"

Erica sensed that Constance wanted to protest, but something seemed to be holding her back. Torn between her desire to explore the mysterious Laramie estate and her growing uncertainty about Jack's intentions, a thousand questions buzzed through Erica's mind, each one more pressing than the last.

"Alright," Erica finally agreed, her curiosity winning out over caution.

She glanced at Constance, seeking reassurance, but found none in the redhead's worried expression.

Chapter Ten

Jack led the way, and as they ventured deeper into the garden, Erica couldn't help but marvel at the extraordinary sculptures that seemed to emerge from the very earth itself. There were nymphs entwined with ivy, cherubs perched on crumbling pedestals, and even a grotesque gargoyle leering down at them from a gnarled oak tree.

"Your work is... impressive," she said cautiously.

Her gaze lingered on a life-sized statue of a young woman whose features appeared almost too perfect to be real.

"Thank you," Jack replied, his voice filled with pride. "I believe in capturing the essence of life in every piece I create."

"Indeed," Erica murmured.

"Shall we continue?" Jack asked, gesturing for them to follow him.

"Perhaps we should head back inside now, Jack," Constance suggested, wringing her hands nervously. "We only came out so far to bury Tiny."

"But the day is still young," Jack chided gently, his smile never quite reaching his eyes.

Erica noticed the subtle shift in Constance's posture, the way her shoulders sagged ever so slightly under the weight of Jack's words. It was clear that something unsaid lingered between them, some secret that granted Jack power.

As they continued their journey through the garden, Erica couldn't help but feel like a pawn in some twisted game, but there was something about Jack's insistence that made it impossible to side with Constance and head back to the house.

"Here we are," he announced.

He led them into a secluded grove where a breathtaking sculpture of an angel towered above them. Its wings were spread wide, as if preparing to take flight, and its face held a sorrowful expression that seemed to transcend time itself.

"Isn't she magnificent?" Jack coaxed.

For a moment, all Erica could do was nod, the statue's beauty rendering her speechless. And yet, even as she admired its craftsmanship, she couldn't shake the feeling that something was off about it. The expression was so real, so precise, the agony seeming to radiate from within the body of the stone.

"Ah, I almost forgot," Jack said with a sly smile as he led Constance and Erica away. "There's one more thing I'd like to show you."

"Jack, I really think we should head back now," Constance said pleadingly, her voice trembling slightly.

"It's not far," he replied smoothly, ignoring her concerns with ease.

As the three of them made their way through the garden, Constance shot Erica an apologetic look. They eventually reached a tall hedge that seemed to stretch for miles in several directions.

Jack turned to face them, his eyes gleaming with excitement.

"I think you'll like this, Erica," he announced. "The Laramie estate maze."

"Really, Jack?" Constance tried again.

Jack simply shook his head dismissively.

"Enough chatter," he said. "You'll see, it's worth the detour."

With that, he stepped into the maze, leaving Constance and Erica with no choice but to follow.

As they ventured deeper into the labyrinth, the air grew colder and shadows stretched across the narrow pathways. The towering hedges seemed to close in on them, their branches twisted together. Each turn led them further away from the garden and the relative safety of the large house.

The maze seemed to grow more sinister with each passing moment, the sense of being lost and trapped weighing heavily on Erica's mind. As they made their way around, each new statue seemed more haunting than the last; some bore expressions of sorrow and fear, while others appeared almost otherworldly in their beauty.

Suddenly, Jack stopped in his tracks, a triumphant smile playing across his lips.

"I'm particularly proud of this one," he declared, gesturing towards something up ahead.

And there, in the heart of the maze, stood a life-sized statue of a young woman. She was beautiful, her stone face frozen in an expression of serenity, and her hands clasped together as if in prayer. The sunlight filtered through the leaves above, casting small shadows on her delicate features.

"Jack, this is incredible," Erica said, unable to tear her eyes away from the sculpture. "You made this?"

"Indeed," he replied. "She was one of my favourite subjects."

"Who was she?"

"Her name was Lily," Jack answered with a faraway expression. "A lost soul, much like myself, I suppose."

"Oh," Erica mused, a little uncomfortable and surprised by Jack's display of emotion. "What happened to her?"

"Ah, well," Jack said with a sigh, looking deliberately away from the statue. "That's a story for another time, I'm afraid."

"Oh," Erica murmured once more, this time wishing not to pry.

"Anyway," said Jack. "Let's carry on."

The air seemed to thicken as they finally made their way out of the maze. Erica glanced back at the intricate labyrinth that had swallowed them whole, its twists and turns now hidden behind a curtain of greenery.

"Come," Jack beckoned, his voice cutting through the silence like a sharpened blade. "I have something more to show you, Erica – my studio. It's just a short walk from here."

Constance hesitated, her eyes darting between Jack and Erica as if seeking some unspoken permission.

"Jack, I really think we should head back to the house. It's getting late, and..."

"Constance," he cut in abruptly, his gaze fixing on her with intensity. "We're already out here. It would be a shame not to show Erica everything while we have the opportunity."

"Of course," Constance whispered, her shoulders slumping in resigned defeat.

They traversed the garden, and then stopped before a weathered wooden door nestled amongst the foliage. Without saying a word, Jack unlocked it and turned the handle. It creaked open to reveal a dimly lit room filled with sculptures in various stages of completion. Each was a breathtaking vision of grace and beauty. There were women captured in stone, their faces frozen in expressions of joy, sorrow, and serenity. Some were draped in flowing gowns, while others were partially or fully nude, their bodies preserved for eternity in exquisite detail.

"This is my sanctuary," he said, gesturing for Erica to step inside.

Recalling that Constance had previously stated

her preference to avoid the studio entirely, Erica was grateful to notice that she too had crossed the threshold into Jack's space.

Jack's expression was a mixture of pride and something else – like a dark hunger lurking just beneath the surface. He watched Erica closely, as if gauging her reaction to his creations.

"Jack," Erica finally said. "Why do you sculpt these women? What is it about them that draws you in?"

"Ah, Erica," he replied, his intense stare boring into her. "It's their vulnerability that intrigues me – the fragility of life, the fleeting nature of youth and beauty. These women were all lost, forgotten, and I preserve them in stone so that they may be remembered for eternity."

"Oh," said Erica, taken aback by the melancholic candour of Jack's answer.

"Perhaps one day, Erica, I shall sculpt you," he suggested, his voice barely more than a whisper as his gaze lingered on her.

As his words hung heavy in the air, Erica felt the world tilt beneath her feet. A thousand thoughts raced through her mind – fear, fascination, a desperate urge to flee – but she could do nothing but stand there frozen to the spot. In that moment, she felt an icy shiver run down her spine, the foreboding sense of unease returning with a vengeance.

Chapter Eleven

Erica sat on the bed, alone in her room, her heart still heavy from Tiny's burial and her mind still reeling from the unsettling tour of Jack's studio. She leaned back against the plush pillows with a book – which she had retrieved from the library – cradled in her hands. She took in the scent of the musty pages, and lost herself in a whimsical world of pixies and enchanted forests.

As she turned another page, a distant chime echoed down the hall, pulling her attention away from the story. She counted each resounding note. Five. Dinner time. She sighed, her attention still lingering on the colourful illustrations of the magical creatures.

Reluctantly, she closed the book and rose to her feet, her eyes scanning the room one last time before heading out into the hallway. As she walked downstairs, her thoughts drifted to Constance and Robert, their relationship a beacon of light amidst the tension that enveloped the Laramie family.

They seem happy together, she mused as she trailed her hand along the ornate banister, her fingers tracing the intricate woodwork. The thought gave her a small measure of comfort, but it wasn't enough to dispel her concerns about the strange goings-on that she'd witnessed since arriving at the house.

As she reached the dining room, Erica took a deep breath, steeling herself for the upcoming dinner. In the back of her mind, she couldn't help but think about how different everything had felt in Normandy.

A sombre pall hung over the room, the silence punctuated only by the clinking of silverware and the occasional scrape of a chair.

Erica forced a polite smile as she took a seat. Everyone else had started their meal. Before her was a full plate of potatoes, meat and gravy. She could feel Jack's gaze lingering on her, his eyes dark and intense. Trying hard to conceal a shudder of discomfort, she turned her attention to her food, anxious to focus on anything other than the unsettling feeling that gripped her.

"It feels so different without Tiny," said Uncle Frank to no one in particular, his voice thick with sadness.

"Frank, don't," Aunt Petra said, her tone sharp as she shot her husband a disapproving glance. "It won't help to dwell on it."

Erica could see the pain flash across her uncle's face, but he quickly masked it and returned to his meal. The tension within the family seemed to grow thicker, the air heavy with unspoken emotions.

"Well, everyone," Aunt Petra announced as soon as she'd finished her meal, pushing her chair back and rising to her feet. "I think I shall retire early tonight."

"Me too," said Constance as soon as her mother had left the room. "Robert will be waiting for me to say goodnight."

"Of course, dear," Uncle Frank said with a gracious bow of his head, offering his daughter a warm smile. "Give him our regards."

As Constance slipped away, Jack rose from his seat without a word, his enigmatic demeanour only adding to the mystery that seemed to surround him. Erica felt relieved as she watched him leave the table and head off to a different room.

"Erica," Uncle Frank began, drawing her attention back to him. "I know this house can be overwhelming at times, and I don't want you to feel alone. Would you like to join me for a drink? I have an extensive whisky collection I'd love to share with you."

Erica hesitated, her memories of whisky limited to a few sips during past Christmas celebrations. She didn't particularly enjoy the taste, but she couldn't bear the thought of spending the evening alone in her room, haunted by the strange occurrences that had plagued her since her arrival.

"That sounds lovely," she replied, her tone edged with a trace of obligatory politeness. "Thank you."

"Wonderful," said Uncle Frank, seeming pleased that he would have some company for the evening. "I'll lead the way."

They strolled at a leisurely pace through several corridors of the large house. As they entered a small room at the end of a hallway, an intricate piece of furniture caught Erica's attention.

"Behold my pride and joy," Uncle Frank announced.

He then gestured towards a grand whisky cabinet that stood proudly against the far wall. The piece was a magnificent structure, crafted from rich mahogany and adorned with ornate carvings depicting scenes of mythical creatures intertwined with elaborate foliage. The glass doors were framed by two carved griffins, their wings spread wide as they guarded the treasures within.

"Wow," said Erica as she took in the numerous bottles of various shapes, sizes and colours lining the shelves. "I don't think I've ever seen anything like this before."

"I've spent years collecting these fine whiskies from all over the world," her uncle explained. "Each one has its own unique character and taste."

Eager to please her uncle but feeling somewhat

out of her depth, Erica nodded encouragingly as he began to elaborate on the complexities of the different bottles.

"Here we have a sixteen-year-old Lagavulin from Islay, Scotland," he said, pointing to a dark amber bottle encased in a velvet-lined box. "It has a distinct peaty flavour, with notes of seaweed, brine, and a hint of sweetness."

"Peat?" Erica echoed, trying to recall if she'd ever heard the term before.

"Ah, yes. Peat is a type of soil found in Scotland," Uncle Frank explained, his eyes sparkling with enthusiasm. "It's used in the whisky-making process, giving it that unique earthy taste."

"That's fascinating," Erica murmured, her mind racing to keep up with the wealth of information.

"And this here," he continued, gesturing towards another bottle, "is a rare Japanese whisky – a Yamazaki eighteen-year-old. It's aged in a combination of American oak, Spanish sherry casks, and Japanese Mizunara oak barrels, imparting a beautiful symphony of flavours."

"Wow," was all Erica could manage, feeling increasingly overwhelmed by the intricacies of the whisky world.

As Uncle Frank passionately delved into the specifics of each whisky, Erica found herself admiring his dedication and enthusiasm. Although she didn't understand every detail, she appreciated the depth of his knowledge and the way he shared it with her.

"Here's one I think you'll enjoy," he said.

He selected a bottle from the cabinet and poured a small amount into a delicate glass. He handed it to Erica. She hesitated for a moment before taking a sip, but then allowed the distinctive liquid to roll over her tongue.

"It's about savouring the taste and appreciating the craftsmanship that goes into creating each unique blend," he advised.

Erica nodded, her eyes meeting her uncle's warm gaze. She knew she didn't fully grasp the complexities of the whiskies he so loved, but she was grateful for his company and the opportunity to learn something new.

"Try this one," he suggested, his eyes twinkling with excitement as he picked out a particular bottle from the grand whisky cabinet. "It's an Irish single malt – smooth and easy on the palate."

Erica hesitated for a moment, her hand hovering above the delicate glass that he had poured for her. The amber liquid seemed to glow in the subtle light of the room. Unsure of what to expect, she took a sip, allowing the warmth to spread down her throat and through her chest.

"That's lovely," she murmured, surprised by the pleasant taste.

"I thought you might like it, my dear," he replied, his expression alight with pride as he poured her another generous measure. "Now, remember – savour it, don't rush."

As Erica took another slow sip, he glanced up at the ornate clock on the wall.

"Good heavens," he stated. "Would you look at the time! I really must be off to bed."

Erica agreed, setting her glass down on a nearby table.

With a kind smile, Uncle Frank bid her goodnight and left the room. As she made her way up to the third floor of the mansion alone, the grand staircase creaked beneath her feet, each step echoing through the silent, shadowy halls. Though she hated to acknowledge it, she had a feeling that unseen eyes were watching her every move.

***

Once in her room, Erica slipped between the cool bedsheets, willing herself to relax after the eventful day. Just as her eyelids began to grow heavy, a sudden breeze rustled the curtains, sending them billowing like ghostly apparitions. Her pulse raced, but she forced herself to take slow, deep breaths, reminding herself that it was just the wind.

"Erica..."

No! It can't be!

She could have sworn that she'd just heard a male voice whispering her name – the same one that had taunted her on her first night in the house. The sound was so vivid and terrifying that she couldn't help but scream.

Aunt Petra burst into the room, her features twisted with annoyance.

"For heaven's sake, child!" she snapped. "Do you plan to wake the entire household every night?"

"Sorry, Aunt Petra," Erica stammered, her cheeks hot with embarrassment. "I... I thought I heard something."

"Just calm yourself, dear. It's been a long day."

Leaving no room for further discussion, with a curt nod, Aunt Petra left the room – so hastily that she didn't even think to close the door.

Just then, Jack appeared in the hallway, his dark eyes searching the room. There was something about his presence that served to heighten Erica's anxiety. He moved closer to stand in the doorway, his unnerving gaze never leaving her face. Neither of them spoke. Then, without a word, he closed the door and walked away, the sound of his footsteps diminishing in the corridor.

Trembling and distressed, Erica pulled the covers tightly over her as she defensively curled up on the mattress. Her thoughts raced, each more worrisome than the last. Had the alcohol truly affected her perception, or was there something more sinister at play? Unable to shrug off the feeling of dread that consumed her, she pulled the covers tighter around her body, seeking solace in their protective embrace.

Perhaps it's just the whisky, she hoped, desperately trying to rationalise her fears.

As she attempted to convince herself, the memory of Jack's relentless gaze lingered in her mind. There was something about him that seemed off, but she couldn't quite put her finger on it.

Get a grip, Erica, she scolded herself, determined not to let her imagination get the better of her. *You're letting this place get to you.*

She took a deep, shaky breath, trying to calm her nerves. Exhaling slowly, she willed herself to relax, focusing on the gentle sound of her own breathing. As her heartbeat gradually returned to its normal rhythm, she began to drift off into a fitful sleep.

to its normal rhythm, she began to drift off into a fitful sleep.

Chapter Twelve

The sun was high in the sky when Erica finally awoke from her deep slumber. She shuddered as she recalled the terror of the male voice that had whispered her name in the night, causing her to scream and rouse Aunt Petra, stern and annoyed. Though mortified by the ordeal, Erica couldn't shake the feeling that the sinister voice was real; it had seemed so purposeful, as if it had been seeking something from her.

As she lay there with the daylight shining onto her pillow through the small gap in the curtains, she remembered the alcohol she'd consumed before going to bed, which had rendered her unable to wake from the nightmare that had followed. In it, a bat had flitted about the room, its leathery wings casting dark shapes on the walls like some twisted puppet show. The creature had moved erratically, evading her attempts to catch it or shoo it away. It had seemed to take pleasure in taunting her, flying close to her face but never quite touching her.

The creature had swooped down upon her, its beady eyes locked onto hers with an almost malevolent intensity. There had been something unusual about it – something sinister and unnerving. It had circled around the room, dominating the entire space before finally settling in a corner and watching Erica with an unblinking stare. Fearful of provoking the creature further, she hadn't dared to move. The bat had seemed almost hypnotic in its gaze, as if trying to wordlessly communicate a message. However, the steady thudding of its wings against the air, and its unearthly presence in the room, had been anything but encouraging.

Maybe it was a vampire, Erica joked to herself in the stark light of day.

Her attempt to look back at the dream with a sense of humour did little to alleviate her discomfort.

Her thoughts were interrupted by a knock at her bedroom door. Before she could muster up a response, Jack opened it, his intense stare focusing on her as he stood in the doorway.

Startled by the sudden and bold intrusion, Erica quickly pulled the covers up to her chin.

"Erica," he said, his voice smooth but unsettling. "It seems everyone else has already busied themselves for the day. I'm the only one at home right now. Would you care to join me in my sculpting studio this afternoon?"

His invitation made her uncomfortable, but with no one else around to consult, Erica felt cornered.

"Oh, um, ok," she answered hesitantly. "Could you give me five minutes to get dressed?"

"Of course," Jack agreed, his tone almost too polite. "I'll have some tea and toast prepared for you so you won't have to walk through the garden on an empty stomach."

His kindness caught her off guard, causing her to scold herself internally for so often thinking the worst of him.

"Thank you," she murmured.

She watched Jack retreat from her room and close the door behind him. She then began to dress, her mind swirling with questions about Jack's intentions and the mysterious dream that had haunted her sleep.

***

The warm sunlight bathed the garden in a golden hue, casting intricate patterns of light and shadow on the gravel path beneath their feet. Erica couldn't help but admire the vibrant colours of the flowers as they swayed gently in the breeze. She inhaled deeply, embracing their sweet fragrance.

"Beautiful, isn't it?" Jack remarked, his voice gentle and charming, drawing her attention back to him.

Despite her lingering discomfort, Erica couldn't deny the beauty surrounding them. The picturesque scene seemed at odds with the sense of dread that gnawed at her insides. She chastised herself for her paranoia and forced a smile.

"Yes, it really is lovely," she replied, trying to match Jack's casual tone.

As they continued towards the sculpting studio, Erica's eyes roamed the landscape, searching for solace in her surroundings. Yet, no matter how hard she tried, she couldn't bury the memory of Jack's earlier words – his desire to sculpt her. The thought sent an involuntary shiver down her spine, and she wrapped her arms around herself, seeking comfort.

"Are you cold?" Jack asked, genuine concern flickering across his face. "We're almost there. My studio has a fireplace – I can light it if you like."

Although Erica graciously thanked Jack, his kindness only served to heighten her concerns. There was something about his mannerisms that didn't quite sit right; he was too polite, too charming. She couldn't get past the feeling that it was all a carefully-crafted façade.

As they approached the sculpting studio, the sun's rays filtering through the trees seemed to lose their warmth, leaving the air around them heavy with tension. As Jack opened the door and gestured for her to enter, Erica hesitated, her pulse quickening.

"Please, make yourself at home," he said, his

voice inviting and tender.

Underneath Jack's veneer of politeness, Erica detected a dark undercurrent that sent a jolt of anxiety coursing through her entire body. Nevertheless, she felt unable to object.

"Your work is incredible," she admitted as she stepped over the threshold, hopeful that offering an honest complement would lighten the mood.

"Thank you," Jack replied, a hint of pride creeping into his voice as he closed the studio door behind him. "I hope that one day, I can capture your essence just as effectively."

The remark reignited Erica's fears. She struggled to maintain her composure. She knew she needed to keep her wits about her, but the conflicting emotions swirling within left her feeling unsteady, uncertain of how to proceed.

She could feel her heart thumping as she desperately searched for a response, but before she could think of one, the studio door burst open with a loud bang to reveal Mrs McGinnon. Standing in the doorway, the housekeeper's face seemed flushed, her eyes wide with worry.

"I apologise for my intrusion," Mrs McGinnon announced, addressing Jack with urgency. "There has been a small fire in the kitchen. The rest of the family is still out, and I believe it's only right that you come immediately to inspect the damage."

Erica noticed that Jack seemed livid about Mrs McGinnon's sudden appearance, his jaw clenched and nostrils flaring.

"Very well," he responded through gritted teeth. "I'd better go and take a look."

Chapter Thirteen

Back at the house, Jack stormed furiously towards the kitchen, with Erica and Mrs McGinnon trailing behind. Just before they reached their destination, he turned to them abruptly, his voice terse.

"Leave me alone while I inspect the kitchen. I don't need an audience for this."

Mrs McGinnon frowned, but did not protest. Instead, she gently took Erica's arm and guided her away from Jack, leading her upstairs. As they walked, Erica found herself grateful for the housekeeper's presence. In the midst of the confusion, the older woman's maternal care provided her with a small measure of comfort.

Mrs McGinnon led the way into Erica's bedroom, and then, once they were inside, she closed the door behind her and leaned in close to Erica, urgency written all over her face.

"Listen closely, dear," she whispered, her voice shaking with emotion. "I couldn't let you be alone with Jack. I had to create a diversion, so I caused the smallest of fires in the kitchen."

Erica's eyes widened as she realised the extent of Mrs McGinnon's concern for her safety. How dangerous could Jack really be if she'd taken such drastic measures to keep them apart?

"Mrs McGinnon, why would you do that?" Erica asked, her anxiety heightening with every word. "What do you know about Jack that I don't?"

"Erica, there are things about this family that..."

Mrs McGinnon's words were cut off by a sharp knock at the door.

"Mrs McGinnon?" Aunt Petra called out from the hallway, her stern tone leaving no room for argument. "I'd like a word with you, please!"

"Of course, Madam," Mrs McGinnon replied.

As the housekeeper shakily opened the door,

before stepping out to face her employer, she looked back at Erica for a moment, her eyes full of unspoken warnings.

Erica remained in her room, her mind racing as she listened to Aunt Petra and Mrs McGinnon walk away, their voices too distant to decipher. It made her feel guilty to think that Mrs McGinnon could be facing severe consequences for the fire.

***

Erica spent the next couple of hours in her room, worrying and unable to relax enough to read her book. By the time she went down for dinner, the atmosphere in the Laramie household had shifted. As she took her seat at the dining table, she couldn't help but notice how Aunt Petra, Uncle Frank and Constance seemed completely indifferent about the fire. Although Erica was relieved to think that Mrs McGinnon wasn't in trouble, the family's nonchalance only served to heighten her discomfort and confusion.

As they ate in relative silence, Erica glanced over at Jack, who sat quietly, his jaw clenched and his eyes fixed on her. With his sinister gaze burning into her like hot coals, she couldn't help but feel that he was harbouring a secret rage towards both her and Mrs McGinnon.

"Jack," Uncle Frank said suddenly, bringing Erica out of her thoughts. "Thank you for attending to everything today."

"I didn't have a choice," he replied curtly, his eyes still fixed on Erica.

Erica swallowed hard as she tried to piece together the puzzle before her. Why did everyone apart from Jack seem so accepting of what had happened in the kitchen? What did they know that she didn't?

As the sun dipped behind the horizon, filling the room with an eerie twilight, Erica sensed that the truth seemed to be lurking just out of reach, casting its dark shadow over the Laramie household.

Chapter Fourteen

The moon was nothing more than a faint sliver in the sky, casting a pale glow through the gap in the curtains. Erica's breaths were shallow and measured as she lay in her bed, entangled in sweat-dampened sheets. Her dreams had been plagued by shadows and whispers, leaving her restless.

A creak from the floorboards jolted her into full consciousness. As her eyes adjusted to her surroundings, her heart pounded in her chest like a wild animal caught in a snare. And then, she saw him: Jack – standing at the foot of her bed. Like a figure from a nightmare, he was tall and imposing, his form shrouded in darkness; only the whites of his eyes gleamed in the dim light.

"J-Jack?" she stammered, her voice barely above a whisper.

Panic rose in her throat like bile. She wanted to run, but she was too scared to move, or even scream.

"Shhh," he urged convincingly.

He moved with unnatural swiftness, and before Erica knew what was happening, he had clamped a hand over her mouth, his fingers icy cold, his grip unyielding and almost suffocating.

"You mustn't scream, Erica," he whispered, fully in control. "You have no idea what I'm capable of."

Wide-eyed with terror, all Erica could do was frantically nod her head, feeling the tears prick at the corners of her eyes. Satisfied that she would keep quiet, Jack removed his hand, leaving her gasping for air.

"Good girl," he murmured.

He then circled the bed to slide under the covers beside her. The mattress dipped beneath his weight, pressing her into the edge of the bed. He moved closer still. With no space between them, she could feel the strange chill emanating from his body.

"Jack, please," she choked out between shallow breaths.

She tried to twist away, but found herself trapped within his firm grip around her waist.

"Quiet," he admonished, his breath tickling her ear as he spoke. "I've been desperate to sculpt you in my studio, Erica. But it seems that everyone wants to keep me from my muse."

A feeling of nausea washed over Erica as she listened to his words, each one feeling like a dagger to her chest. What could he want with her? Why was he here, invading the sanctity of her room in the dead of night?

"Since everyone seems so set on keeping you away from me," Jack continued, his voice barely audible above the pounding of her heartbeat, "I've decided to try a different strategy to spend some quality time with you."

He paused for a moment, letting the full weight of his intentions sink in. Erica could feel the sweat trickling down her spine as her blood ran colder than the night outside.

"Jack," she whispered, her voice trembling with

fear. "Why are you doing this?"

"Because, Erica," he replied, his breath hot on her neck, "you are a work of art that I cannot resist."

Erica desperately wanted to get away, but she was too shocked and afraid to move.

"Your skin..." he murmured as he nuzzled in closer towards her. "It's so soft and tender."

"Please, Jack," she begged, her voice barely audible. "Please don't hurt me."

He paused, his lips brushing against her ear for a lingering moment.

"Hurt you?" he whispered. "No, Erica. I don't want to hurt you. I want to love you."

This startled her. She had never considered that Jack could harbour such feelings for her. She had always assumed he preferred solitude, consumed in his mysterious ways.

"Love me?" she managed to whisper.

"Yes," he replied, his voice laced with longing.

"I've loved before. I've sculpted their beauty just as I long to sculpt yours. Lily, for instance."

Erica thought back to the statue of Lily in the garden maze, its lifelike features a testament to Jack's skill. But there was something darker lurking behind his confession. She needed to know more.

"Jack, what happened to Lily?" she asked hesitantly, afraid of the answer.

He sighed, his breath ghosting along her neck.

"Lily..." he said wistfully. "She died. One night, I made her too weak. I drained her of too much blood."

"Blood?!" Erica exclaimed, her eyes wide with horror. "What do you mean?"

"Drinking a woman's blood feels natural to me, Erica," Jack confessed, his voice tinged with a sadistic edge. "Because I loved her. And because... I'm a vampire."

The revelation hit Erica like a ton of bricks. Jack, a vampire? It was almost too much to comprehend. She couldn't help herself –

escaping his grip with strength fuelled by sheer emotion, she scrambled off the bed, backing away from it as her whole body shook with terror.

"Get away from me!" she whispered frantically, her voice wavering with fear.

"Erica," he implored, his eyes dark and intense. "There's nothing to worry about. I won't hurt you. I promise."

But she could see it in his eyes: that predatory hunger that lurked beneath his words. And she knew that, despite his promise, she was anything but safe.

With his gaze fixed on her, Jack rolled gracefully off the bed and confidently stood up.

Daunted that he was stood just metres away from her, his glare intense and unrelenting, Erica's breath came in shallow gasps as sweat beaded on her brow. She continued to back away from Jack, her fear palpable. The way he looked at her, the way his eyes gleamed with a dark hunger – it was too much. She had to find something, anything, that she could use to protect herself.

Desperation fuelled her racing thoughts, and as she glanced around the room, her eyes landed upon a small gold cross hanging from a necklace on the dressing table. With a surge of adrenaline, she lunged for it. Clutching the cross tightly in her trembling fingers, she then held it out towards Jack like a shield.

"Stay back!" she warned, her voice low and quivering with terror. "Don't come any closer!"

Jack merely laughed, an unsettling sound that sent chills down her spine.

"Oh, Erica," he taunted, stepping closer despite her protests. "You really believe that old wives' tale about vampires being vulnerable to crosses and garlic? How endearingly naive."

The realisation that her makeshift weapon was useless hit her hard, leaving her feeling even more vulnerable and frightened. But she couldn't give up – she had to do something to escape.

"Get away from me," she whispered, her voice raw with fear as she began to back towards the bedroom door.

His movements slow and deliberate, Jack continued to walk towards her until the distance between them was merely a metre. It caused Erica to shudder.

"Disgusted by me, are you?" he said with a snarl, clearly infuriated by the rejection.

Immediately, his face twisted into a ghastly visage, fangs baring and black nails elongating as he seemed to grow unnaturally taller.

Forgetting his earlier warning, Erica let out a piercing scream as the true horror of Jack's identity became clear. This was no longer a strange and mysterious man – this was a monster.

The oppressive silence of the night now shattered, Aunt Petra and Uncle Frank burst into the room. Their mouths hung open at the sight before them: Erica, her eyes wide with terror, and Jack, his transformation all too real.

"Jack! Stop this at once!" Aunt Petra commanded, her voice shaking with anger.

Erica's jaw dropped wide open as she realised that not only was Jack a vampire, but that Aunt

Petra seemed to already know about his true nature. Had they all been hiding this terrible secret from her?

Jack let out a nonchalant laugh, his sinister grin filled with malice. The transformation continued, his monstrous form becoming more pronounced as he stalked even closer towards Erica. Her breath hitched in her throat as dread clawed at her chest.

"Jack, we had an agreement," Aunt Petra reminded him, her eyes pleading for him to stop. "You were to leave Erica alone."

"Ha! I don't care about any agreement," he said with spite, his fangs gleaming dangerously. "I want Erica, and I'm going to have her."

"B-but..." Aunt Petra stammered.

"Killing Tiny should have been enough to lure Erica into my studio," Jack said cunningly, his eyes flickering with dark amusement as he revealed the true extent of his obsession. "I thought I'd set up the perfect ruse to get Erica up to that end of the garden when we went there to bury the poor dog."

"Tiny?" said Uncle Frank, his voice thick with betrayal and grief. "You killed Tiny? I thought you cared for him!"

"Oh, but I did," Jack purred, his gaze never leaving Erica's terrified face. "But my desire to bring Erica into my world far outweighed my compassion for that little creature."

"Please, Jack," Erica begged helplessly. "Please don't hurt me."

But Jack's cruel laughter only grew louder as he closed in on her, the promise of darkness and pain etched across his twisted features.

In that moment, Constance and Robert burst into the room, their faces a picture of concern and panic.

"Jack," Constance choked out, her voice trembling. "We had an agreement. You were to leave Erica alone."

Erica felt betrayed at the confirmation that Constance and Robert knew about Jack's true nature. The deception stung like daggers of ice, slicing through her already-fragile trust in the Laramie family.

"Enough!" Aunt Petra shouted, her voice laced with desperation as she tried to regain her composure. "Jack, please, we beg of you! Leave Erica be."

"Ah, but where's the fun in that?" he said with a sneer, his eyes alight with malice.

In that instant, he lunged forward and grabbed Erica from behind, his cold fingers digging through her nightgown and into her flesh. She whimpered as he held her firmly, effectively making her his hostage. Silently pleading for help, her eyes searched the faces of everyone at the door.

"Let her go, Jack!" Uncle Frank demanded, his hands balled into fists at his sides. "This has gone too far!"

"I'll be the judge of that," Jack said menacingly as he tightened his grip on Erica, revelling in her fear.

As Erica struggled against Jack, her thoughts raced with the knowledge that everyone in the room had known about him being a vampire. They had all kept this dark secret from her, leaving her vulnerable to the monster that now held her captive.

"Please," she whispered, tears streaming down her cheeks. "Don't hurt me."

"Quiet now, my dear," Jack cooed, his voice dripping with venom. "You're mine, and there's nothing anyone can do to change that."

"Let me go!" she screamed, her voice hoarse from the agonising torment.

Immediately, the room's atmosphere shifted. Mrs McGinnon, with the aggression and determination of a mother swan fighting to defend her young, burst in. Held tightly in her white-knuckled hand was one of Jack's smaller sculptures. Erica held her breath as her would-be saviour charged towards the vampire.

"Get away from her, you monster!" Mrs McGinnon roared angrily, her eyes blazing with stark conviction.

With precision, she swung the heavy sculpture at Jack's head, the impact resounding throughout the room. In a state of shock, he loosened his grip on Erica. It was just enough for her to slip away from him. She scrambled back, her eyes locked on the scene unfolding before her.

Jack's eyes filled with disbelief and fury as a trickle of blood began to seep from the gash on his forehead. It dripped down, shockingly crimson against his pale skin as he continued to glare in wanting at Erica. For a moment, time seemed to slow down, the world holding its breath as everyone waited to see what would happen next.

Then, when the full force of the blow finally registered, Jack let out an unearthly scream that caused everyone to recoil in shock. His body convulsed violently before disintegrating into a thick vapour that swirled around the room like a violent storm. As quickly as it had appeared, the ominous cloud vanished, leaving behind nothing more than a fine layer of ash and the lingering stench of death.

Chapter Fifteen

The following day, everyone gathered together in the lounge, shadows of their former selves. Aunt Petra and Uncle Frank had their own large armchairs, whilst Mrs McGinnon sat perched on a wooden stool. On a velvet-lined sofa, Constance was sat next to Robert, her hand laced in his. She looked compassionately at Erica, who stood leaning against a pristine windowsill, the early morning sun highlighting the exhaustion and shock on her features.

Aunt Petra spoke first, her voice steady despite the weight of her words.

"We've always known about Jack being a vampire," she admitted, her eyes meeting Erica's in a silent plea for understanding. "He wasn't our son. Our only child is Constance. Jack... he attached himself to our family decades ago, and we had no choice but to comply with his demands."

"We thought that if we kept him happy, and provided him with a studio to work from, he would leave us alone," Uncle Frank explained. "We always feared him, but we never imagined he would go this far."

The sadness that seemed etched into her uncle's features now made sense to Erica – he and his family had been living under the constant threat of a monster.

"Why didn't any of you tell me?" Erica asked, her tone direct with anger and hurt. "I had a right to know!"

"Jack had forbidden us from telling anyone," Aunt Petra confessed, wringing her hands together. "But we should have warned you somehow. We could see it in his eyes when he looked at you... we knew he wanted you."

"I tried to warn you on the way here," Robert chimed in, his expression full of regret. "I was certain that you'd be his type. All the same though, the risk of breaking Jack's trust was far too high. You now know what he was capable of."

Gracefully acknowledging Robert's words, Erica nodded sadly before turning to face Mrs McGinnon.

"Thank you, Mrs McGinnon," she said sincerely, her voice choked with emotion. "I don't know what would have happened if you hadn't stepped in."

"You're more than welcome, dear," Mrs McGinnon replied, her kind smile reassuring and warm. "I just did what I had to do."

Aunt Petra, Uncle Frank, Constance and Robert exchanged looks – all tainted with guilt and shame. Nobody could deny that if it wasn't for Mrs McGinnon's quick thinking and bravery, Erica could have suffered a terrible fate. Nevertheless, they were clearly relieved that Jack's reign of terror had come to an end.

"A part of me feels terrible in saying so," said Aunt Petra, her tone serious, "but Jack was such a recluse, and so elusive most of the time, that I doubt anyone beyond the estate will even notice that he's gone."

"It's probably for the best," said Uncle Frank.

Everyone hastily agreed.

Aunt Petra leaned forward in her chair, her expression suddenly soft with genuine gratitude.

"You know, Erica, in a strange way, we should be thanking you. If it wasn't for your arrival, Jack might still be alive and controlling us."

"I didn't do anything," Erica replied, unable to accept the praise. "It was all Mrs McGinnon."

"Perhaps," Robert agreed, the weight of their ordeal still etched deeply into his features. "But sometimes it takes an outsider to shed light on our darkest secrets and show us that change is necessary."

"Indeed," said Uncle Frank, his voice rough with unspoken emotions. "Erica's presence here has given us an opportunity to finally confront our fears and put an end to this nightmare."

"Whatever the reason," Constance chimed in, her eyes shining with a newfound determination, "we now have a chance to rebuild our lives and become a family again. No more pretending. No more fear."

"Here's to new beginnings," Aunt Petra declared, raising an imaginary toast.

The others smiled, echoing her sentiment as they basked in the warmth of the moment.

As Erica looked around the room, she was confident that everyone was on the precipice of a new chapter. It was as though the heavy atmosphere in the house was lifting, to be replaced by a tentative sense of hope and healing. No longer subservient to darkness personified, everyone was now free to rebuild their lives.

www.ingramcontent.com/pod-product-compliance
Lightning Source LLC
Chambersburg PA
CBHW031252210726
48287CB00003B/999